The Mystery of the Maya

Maya

Uncovering the Lost City of Palenque

Peter Lourie

Boyds Mills Press

For the Morales family

Acknowledgments

Excavations at Palenque in the Cross Group and Southern Acropolis took place under the auspices of the Palenque Project, which is a joint venture of the Precolumbian Art Research Institute (PARI) and Mexico's Instituto Nacional de Antropología e Historia (INAH). Directed by Merle Greene Robertson and principal investigator Alfonso Morales Cleveland, this multidisciplinary project was staffed by an international group of archaeologists and other specialists in the study of the ancient Maya. Many thanks to Alfonso Morales for letting me wander at will through the ruins during this time of great discovery, and also to Chris Powell, the field director of the excavations.

Funding for Ed Barnhart's mapping came from FAMSI—Foundation for the Advancement of Mesoamerican Studies, Inc.—which is based in Florida. None of the fine work at Palenque, neither the excavations nor the mapping, would be possible without the generous permission of Mexico's INAH. The permit from INAH was granted to PARI, which works in coordination with other nonprofit organizations.

Many thanks to the following contributors:

Jorge Pérez de Lara: cover (front left/right), pages 3, 9 (bottom), 13, 18 (top right/bottom right), 19, 30 (bottom), 31.

Erich Lessing/Art Resource, NY: front cover (center), page 9 (top).

Randall F. Llewellyn: map page 6.

Petra Fine Art: page 8 (engraving by Frederick Catherwood).

Justin Kerr: page 10 (right).

Library of Congress: page 15.

Image reproduced from the facsimile edition of Biología Centrali-Americana by Alfred Percival Maudslay. Published 1974 by Milpatron Publishing Corp., Stamford, CT 06902. Further reproduction prohibited: page 16 (left).

Ed Barnhart: map page 22.

Boyds Mills Press, Inc.
A Highlights Company
815 Church Street
Honesdale, Pennsylvania 18431
Printed in China

U.S. Cataloging-in-Publication Data
    (Library of Congress Standards)

Lourie, Peter.
    The mystery of the Maya : uncovering the lost city of Palenque / written and photographed by Peter Lourie. —1st edition.
[48]p. : col. Ill. (maps) ;   cm.
Includes index.
Summary: Chronicle of a journey to the Maya ruins of Palenque, Mexico.
1. Mexico — Antiquities. 2. Mayas — Antiquities. 3. Palenque Site (Mexico). I. Title.
972.75 21 2001   AC   CIP
00-103739

ISBN 1-56397-839-3 HC 1-59078-265-8 PB

First edition, 2001
First Boyds Mills Press paperback edition, 2004

Book designed by Randall F. Llewellyn
Book coordinated by Rebecca J. Ent
Book edited by Greg Linder, Linder Creative Services
The text of this book is set in 12-point Hiroshige Medium.

10 9 8 7 6 5 4 3 2   HC
10 9 8 7 6 5 4 3 2 1 PB

The beauty of the sculpture, the solemn stillness of the woods, disturbed only by the scrambling of the monkeys and the chattering of parrots, the desolation of the city, and the mystery that hung over it, all created an interest higher, if possible, than I had ever felt among the ruins of the old world.

— John L. Stephens
Author and early explorer of Palenque

A Deadly Snake

The fer-de-lance was dead but still moving.

My first day in the Mexican jungle, the howler monkeys roared all around us. Moths as big as bats fluttered through the faded green light under the forest canopy. I had been in the jungle for only an hour when Rogelio Lopez, one of two *macheteros* who had been hired to cut through the thick vegetation, chopped off the head of a snake with his long machete. When the macheteros burst into shouts, I ran to see the headless form of a fer-de-lance on the jungle floor. The snake was dead, but it was still moving. Rogelio hung the carcass on a stick as a warning to all who passed through the area.

The fer-de-lance is one of the most poisonous snakes in Central America and this part of Mexico. Gray with black-edged diamonds running down its back and named by the French for its lance-shaped head, this pit viper can grow up to eight feet long. Its bite all but guarantees a quick death. Descendants of the Maya say that if you are bitten by a fer-de-lance, only a shaman can save your life.

I was frightened by the encounter with the snake. I had flown from Vermont, a northern state where venomous snakes are rarely seen, to the southern

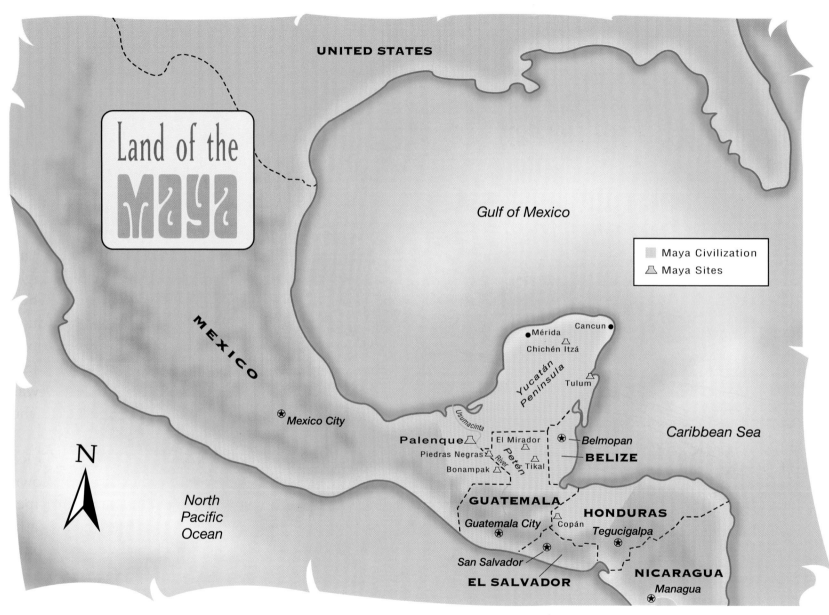

Land of the Maya

UNITED STATES

Gulf of Mexico

Maya Civilization
Maya Sites

M E X I C O

Mérida
Cancun
Chichén Itzá

Yucatán Peninsula

Tulum

Mexico City

Caribbean Sea

Usumacinta

Palenque
El Mirador
Belmopan
Piedras Negras
River
BELIZE
Petén
Bonampak
Tikal

N

GUATEMALA

HONDURAS

North
Pacific
Ocean

Guatemala City
Copán
Tegucigalpa

San Salvador

NICARAGUA

EL SALVADOR
Managua

For hundreds of years, Maya civilization dominated much of Central America and parts of Mexico.

Mexican state of Chiapas on the Guatemalan border. Here I joined Ed Barnhart, an archaeologist who was traipsing through the rain forest to rediscover the ancient Maya city of Palenque. Ed and his macheteros were clearing the vegetation in order to uncover buildings that had been hidden by jungle for more than a thousand years. After my first day in the jungle, I vowed to wear my high rubber boots to protect my legs from snakes.

To the untrained eye, the Maya buildings that Ed is mapping are hard to identify. Neglected for such a long time, they look like piles of stone half-buried in rotting earth. Yet these are the remains of one of the planet's greatest civilizations. The Maya had flourished for hundreds of years until they mysteriously abandoned their cities. Even today, no one is exactly sure why they left.

I had come to Mexico thinking the Maya culture had been thoroughly studied. I knew the Maya had built cities without knowing how to use the wheel or metal tools. I knew they had devised a complex system of writing, had developed sophisticated calendars, and could predict movements of the sun, moon, and planets. I imagined that most of their hieroglyphs had been translated, and that all of their temples and tombs had been explored.

I was wrong.

As many as two thousand structures have lain untouched for a thousand years at Palenque.

When Ed and I walked through what was once the main plaza of Palenque, I saw unexplored temples standing right next to excavated ones. During more than a hundred years of excavating, fewer than forty structures had been uncovered. As Ed surveys and maps the outlying regions of the city, he is discovering that as many as two thousand structures may have lain untouched for a millennium in this remote jungle.

This engraving by British artist Frederick Catherwood shows the Palace at Palenque as it appeared in the mid-nineteenth century.

The ancient Maya created jade masks and stone sculptures.

The Mystery of Maya History

The Classic Maya period lasted from around A.D. 250 until A.D. 900. During this time, the Maya people built beautiful cities with temples, palaces, pyramids, and plazas. Religious ceremonies, feasts, affairs of government, and commerce drew thousands of outlying residents to the city centers. There were more than fifty independent city-states on the Yucatán Peninsula during the Classic period.

Around A.D. 900, however, the great civilization faltered. The Maya stopped building sacred structures and abandoned their cities altogether. Experts think this could have resulted from overpopulation, war, or environmental damage. It is likely that the people left the cities to migrate northward, in search of better farmland.

Later, another phase of Maya civilization developed in the northern sections of the Yucatán Peninsula. But the arrival of Spanish conquerors in the sixteenth century brought this phase to a sudden end, too.

Much of what we now know about the Maya comes to us through their art and hieroglyphic writings. Their writings have been found on ancient pottery, ornaments, stone monuments, and temple walls.

Sophisticated stone figures adorn the walls of the Palace at Palenque.

The Maya Universe

The Maya believed in many gods, among them the god of rain and the god of corn. They also believed that the universe contained three worlds, or layers of life. At the bottom, below the earth, was the Underworld. It was called Xibalbá. This was a world of death, a frightening place containing dark spirits, powerful gods, and rotting flesh.

In the middle was the earth, or Middleworld, the place inhabited by the living Maya. The Maya thought of the earth as a giant crocodile or turtle floating on a sea.

The world above the floating earth was the Heavens, where invisible but powerful gods resided. The Maya attempted to communicate with their gods through animal sacrifice, prayer, and visions.

To the Maya, all things were alive. Trees, rocks, and animals were imbued with spirits. A giant tree called the ceiba tree was sacred because the Maya believed this tree connected all three layers of the universe. The roots

The face of Hun Hun Ahpu, Maya Corn God, appears on this pottery bowl.

of the ceiba went deep into the Underworld. The trunk of the ceiba passed through the Middleworld, and the foliage swept the Heavens. The Maya called the ceiba the Tree of Life, or the World Tree.

Kings and Priests

Maya kings ruled on matters of war, government, and commerce. The people believed their rulers were divine beings who could communicate with the gods. Like the Tree of Life, the kings connected the Maya people to the world of the supernatural.

Everyone, from the kings to the common people, cut themselves to make blood flow. They believed blood-letting triggered personal visions that contained important messages from the Heavens. In order to make decisions about a war, for example, a king might cover the bark of a tree with his own blood and then burn the bark. Out of the smoke, a vision might emerge that would help the king win the war.

The Maya believed that gods and people needed each other. Gods needed people to worship and nourish them. People needed gods to help bring rain and create new life. Because the Maya believed their survival depended entirely on the gods, religion dominated everyday activity. Priests guided the Maya people through many rituals. On special religious occasions, the priests directed ceremonies that might involve dancing, praying, feasting, sacrificing animals, and the letting of blood from human flesh. The Maya believed they could nourish the gods with human blood, and that this would make the gods happy. If the gods were content, life for the Maya would also be good.

The author stands before a ceiba tree, called the Tree of Life by the ancient Maya.

The Maya Today

Today, the Maya people are as numerous as they were a thousand years ago. More than six million Maya live in Central America and Mexico. Today's Maya speak not one but many languages. Although they no longer live in city-states or follow the rulings of kings, they maintain many of their ancestors' beliefs. The conquering Spaniards tried to destroy much of their culture, demanding that the Maya speak Spanish and adopt the religious practice of Catholicism. But the cross that Jesus Christ died on reminds many Maya of the sacred Tree of Life. They associate Jesus with the sun and Mother Mary with the moon. In Maya communities today, the people regard the mountains and hills as the homes of deities that watch over humans.

A City Rediscovered

Palenque was known as L'akam Ha, or "Big Water."

Archaeologists believe Palenque was home to as many as ten thousand people. Citizens called their city *L'akam Ha*, or "Big Water," because numerous crystal-clear streams flow out of the ground here. Palenque was built at the edge of the Chiapas Mountains, overlooking a wide coastal plain that stretches north a hundred miles to the Gulf of Mexico.

According to hieroglyphs discovered in the area, Palenque began to flourish in A.D. 431 and lasted until A.D. 799, a period of 368 years. Then, almost overnight, the people abandoned it. Within decades, the city was overgrown by jungle, sinking from view like a stone in water.

When I followed Ed and his mapping crew through the dense rain forest, I witnessed firsthand how a jungle can swallow something as big as a city.

Count Waldek lived in this temple for two years, creating drawings of the city filled with ghosts and spirits.

First Sightings

The outside world knew very little about Maya civilization or L'akam Ha until the first large-scale excavations were begun here in the 1800s. Earlier, a few explorers had passed through the area, but little came of these visits.

In the sixteenth century, the famed Spanish conquistador Hernando Cortés passed within thirty miles of the ruins but did not find them. In 1773, Maya looters told Spanish priests about stone palaces lying in the jungle. One priest led an expedition to Palenque. He was so impressed by the grandeur of the city that he claimed it for Spain, believing it was the capital of the fabled lost continent of Atlantis.

In 1786 Antonio del Río, a Spanish army captain who was stationed in Guatemala, reached Palenque. He and eighty men spent sixteen days clearing the jungle around the ancient city. The buildings had been reduced to rubble, and the jungle was so thick that the men could hardly see beyond a few feet. But as del Río cleared the forest, he began to appreciate the city's former magnificence. The army captain filed a report, which included drawings, but it was forgotten until a British company published the report in England in 1822. After this, interest in the ancient city grew.

In 1831, an eccentric adventurer in his sixties named Count Waldek reached Palenque. Waldek decided to live in one of the temples. He stayed for two years, creating fantastical drawings that showed the city inhabited by ghosts and spirits.

This Catherwood engraving depicts excavations at a Maya temple. Catherwood and Stephens are shown in coats, holding a measuring tape.

Stephens, Catherwood, and Maudslay

The American explorer John L. Stephens came to Palenque a few years later, accompanied by the British artist Frederick Catherwood. Together they explored the site, recording in words and drawings what they found. Upon seeing Maya ruins for the first time, Stephens wrote: "All was mystery, dark, impenetrable mystery. . . ."

When Stephens and Catherwood entered the palace courtyard for their first dinner, Stephens

At left, photographer Alfred P. Maudslay stands in the tower of the Palace. Above, more than a century later, Ed Barnhart stands in the same tower, which has been restored.

plucked two-foot-long leaves to use as a tablecloth. The explorers slept in what had once been a magnificent stone structure, but now the wind blew through holes in the crumbled walls. It kept them from lighting candles, but Stephens wrote that the "darkness of the palace was lighted up by fireflies of extraordinary size and brilliancy, shooting through the corridors . . . forming a beautiful and striking spectacle." The early Spaniards had described these same jungle fireflies as among the wonders of the world, providing so much light that visitors could travel at night.

When Stephens undertook Palenque's first major excavation, he discovered a miraculous aqueduct system that had once carried water throughout the city. Stephens and Catherwood published a book about their explorations throughout the Yucatán, and their book sparked the imagination of the world.

The English photographer Alfred P. Maudslay came to Palenque in the late 1800s. He produced many wonderful photographs and drawings of the city and its monuments. He, too, cleared the jungle and supervised excavations. But today, even though archaeologists have been studying this city for more than a hundred years, they have excavated only thirty-two buildings. As Ed was finding out, thousands more await exploration.

A portion of the ancient aqueduct system that supplied Palenque's drinking water

Palenque: Jewel of the Jungle

These figures appear on the throne of one of Palenque's last kings.

Today, the ruins of the once-great buildings of Palenque sit in the dim jungle light like untold secrets. An American archaeologist named Chris Powell described L'akam Ha to me as "the jewel of the jungle." Chris was the field director in charge of excavations in the ancient city.

"Every archaeologist wants to work at Palenque," Chris told me. Whenever he talked about this magical place—and especially when he described the city in its heyday—his eyes watered and his sentences speeded up, reflecting his excitement. "Palenque was known as the 'red city.' Over the stone walls you see today, there would have been a thick layer of stucco, painted a cinnabar red with highlights of blue, yellow, and white. Water flowed everywhere at Palenque, channeled by one of the most sophisticated aqueduct systems anywhere in the world."

Chris was in the midst of a wonderful period of discovery. At Temple 19 a few months before my arrival, he and his crew had uncovered the throne of one of the last kings of Palenque. On the side of the throne, which had been buried for a thousand years, they found sophisticated Maya art. Long hieroglyphic passages from the throne were now being translated by epigraphers, scientists who study ancient languages. At nearby Temple 20, his crew had opened up perhaps the earliest tomb in the whole city, and Chris was about to begin exploring it.

A captive scorpion

Manuel hacked through the jungle with his machete.

Drawing the Past

While Chris and project director Alfonso Morales excavated methodically day by day, Ed and his mapping crew were finding new terraces and courtyards as they hacked their way up nearby hills.

A Maya legend relates that after two mythological heroes had worked the earth and planted corn, they decided to rest for the day. When they returned to their field the following morning, they found that the trees had risen once again, and all the earth was as before, as if they had never cultivated the land. This was the voracious jungle environment in which the Maya had flourished, and the same environment now makes Ed's mapping job a challenging one.

I joined Ed and his crew on their daily explorations. Every day we awoke in darkness to the loud, early-morning whine of cicadas. We saw three-inch-long scorpions hanging on the walls of our rooms. I captured one scorpion in a coffee can, so I could take it home to my son. Before I had left Vermont, my six-year-old had asked me to bring home a scorpion from the jungle. "Please, Dad, alive, Dad, alive, okay?!"

One morning after coffee, Ed, his two assistants Jim Eckhardt and Kirk French, and I left the house that Ed had built for archaeologists. We drove to the nearby ruins. It was only seven o'clock, but already the heat and humidity were building fast. Rogelio Lopez and Manuel Cruz, the two macheteros hired to cut the jungle back with their long machetes, met us at the ruins. Rogelio was eighteen. Manuel was sixteen.

As Ed gave instructions about where he wanted to work, the

The burning season filled the skies with smoke.

Jim used sophisticated equipment to survey the jungle.

Maya men quietly held their machetes in their hands and listened intently. Occasionally they smiled, but perhaps they were already a little tired. They had set out in darkness from their home in the mountain village of Naranjo, walking five miles to the ruins this morning. At the end of the day, eight hours from now, they would walk uphill back to Naranjo.

I told them I planned to hike up to their village one of these days. I was looking forward to seeing a small Chiapan village where a hundred families survive off the land, much as their Maya ancestors had done for thousands of years. Each village family has its *milpa,* or farm. Rogelio told me he grew oranges, tobacco, corn, beans, and squash on his milpa. His family also raised pigs, chickens, and cows. Tomorrow, he said, he would do some burning.

I had arrived during the burning season, a time when farmers burn their fields to clear them of trees and unwanted vegetation. The burning season comes when the cut jungle is at its driest, right before the tropical rains begin to fall. Each year in May, the heavens cloud with smoke from hundreds of fires on family milpas.

The six of us headed into the forest to map an ancient city. Before Ed could use the sophisticated survey equipment that allows him to draw buildings and diagram the city the way it once looked, Manuel and Rogelio had to clear away the jungle vegetation. I watched them hack and slice. Sometimes they stopped to sharpen their machetes with a small file. Meanwhile, Ed and his two assistants located the old buildings, paced their lengths and widths, and determined their outside corners.

21

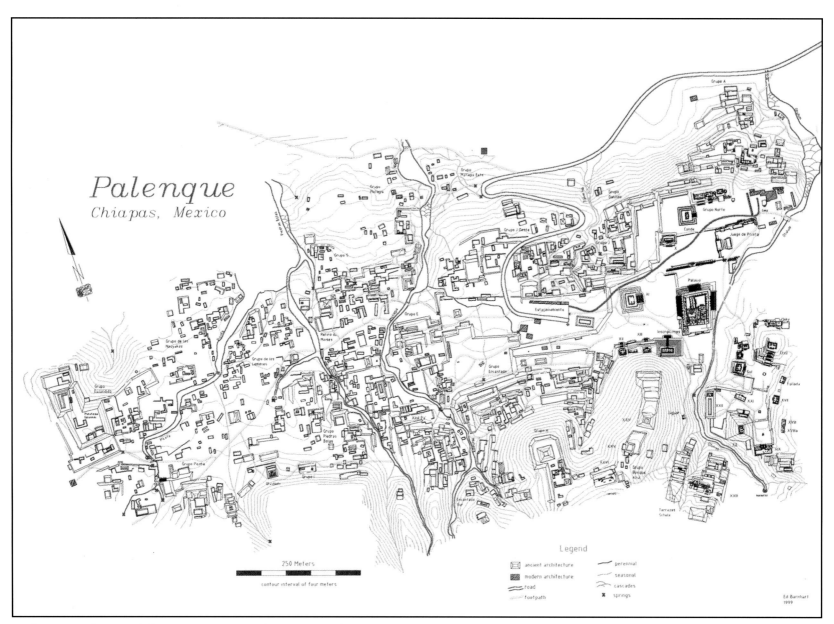

This partial map of the structures at Palenque was drawn and then computerized by Ed Barnhart.

They looked repeatedly at their compasses, which hung around their necks like medallions.

"First we must get the lay of the land and make some preliminary drawings," Ed said. He debated with the others whether one building started here or ended there, and how one structure fit with others. All the while, Ed held a pad and pencil. He drew a crude picture of this portion of the city. As the day got hotter, ancient Palenque began appearing on his graph paper, one building at a time. Out of the mists of time, the Maya were coming back to life.

To do this drawing, and later to map the entire city, requires great physical stamina. The land is far from flat. Palenque was built on a natural terrace, and parts of the city are very steep. The jungle is thick, and there is always the possibility of stepping on a fer-de-lance, a coral snake, or a rattlesnake. Ed told me to watch where I placed my feet and to avoid touching any trees with my hands. Even the littlest trees could be spiky with poisonous thorns.

As Ed drew, the ancient city began to appear on paper.

Many of the small jungle trees are dangerous.

A giant tree grew out of this house mound.

For lunch, Manuel ate pozol *from a bowl.*

The Everyday Maya

For lunch, the crew had peanut butter and jelly sandwiches. Rogelio and Manuel stopped their work to eat from a bowl. They mixed a white corn meal with water to form a mixture called *pozol*. It was a simple food, but it kept them going all day long.

As the crew paced and debated and walked through the ruins, I wandered off, always watching where I placed my feet. In the dim, secret light, I peered at ancient walls that rose out of the earth. At the bottom of tiny streams, the water-sculpted limestone rocks looked man-made. Taking pictures of the half-buried stone, I felt almost dizzy as I floated through this hot, muggy world.

Ed walked up behind me. He told me that many of these structures in the outlying regions of the city were not temples for worship. Instead, they were homes where craftsmen, merchants, and "common folk" had lived. Most of the archaeological work at Palenque had focused on the spiritual center of the city—the Palace, the Temple of the Inscriptions, the Temple of the Sun, and other sacred structures. But Ed was interested in documenting the lives of Palenque's ordinary citizens. He hoped his mapping work would tell us more about the everyday lives of people in the ancient city.

The Temple of the Sun

Looters had come first to this Maya dwelling.

For many years, scientists thought that Maya cities were inhabited by the royal and priestly classes, and that the common folk lived in villages and on farms outside of the city. Most archaeologists believed the people came to city centers only to trade and worship. But Ed's work was painting a different picture.

"We're finding a lot of house mounds," Ed explained. "Look around you. These are Maya homes! There were Maya living here, within the city limits, very close to the ceremonial main plaza."

Ed pointed to a typical Maya dwelling. This house mound had a big, gaping hole on the top, where looters had come years before in search of jade and pottery. It was the custom for the Maya, Ed explained, to bury their dead in their own houses. Alongside the bodies they often buried precious jade for the dead ones to take with them to the afterlife.

Many of the house mounds had huge ceiba trees growing out of their centers like sole survivors from ancient times. The roots of the ceiba trees had grown through roofs and torn the walls apart. Here again was the jungle at work, destroying what was left of the Maya civilization.

The jungle had almost demolished this once-solid wall.

Monkeys in the Suburbs

One day, I heard a special excitement in Ed's voice. As he and his crew hiked higher and higher up the side of a hill, Ed was finding an amazing number of buildings. They just kept appearing, one after another, level after level, in what must have been a major residential area. There seemed no end to the "suburbs" of Palenque.

As the hot day wore on, the howler monkeys started roaring in the distance. The humidity was so high I had to drink a quart of water every few hours. My legs were itching from chigger and mosquito bites. Late in the afternoon, sweat bees added to our discomfort by attacking our faces. A sweat bee seems like a harmless little insect. Each one is about the size of a small fly. They don't sting, but at certain times of day they would come out in swarms to hover relentlessly in our faces. Perhaps, as their name suggests, they are attracted to the salt in perspiration.

In the afternoon, the howlers scrambled overhead for a better look at us. They grew still in the canopy, gazing down with curious, liquid eyes. When John Stephens first heard howlers in the distance, he thought they were lions. Their deep roars sounded angry to me, but Rogelio said they roared only when they were happy.

Howler monkeys came down from the treetops to survey the surveyors.

Archaeologists

Top, Ed demonstrates equipment used to pinpoint the location of structures at Palenque. Below, the surveying crew relaxes at the archaeologists' house before starting their workday.

Like many archaeologists, Ed wanted to be an explorer when he was a kid. For many years, he was fascinated by the Incas of South America. He dreamed of discovering cities hidden in the Andes Mountains of Ecuador. But as a college student, he fell under the spell of the mysterious Maya culture. Ed went to Honduras to work on the ancient Maya city of Copán. He helped reconstruct Maya pottery, and he studied hieroglyphs. He excavated deep inside dark tunnels, breathing mold and the dust from bat feces. While he worked, he faced the constant threat of cave-ins and earthquakes.

"I loved the whole experience," he told me, smiling at the memory. "I loved the people. I loved all the things we didn't know about the Maya." He returned to the United States with hundreds of questions. He wondered who the Maya really were and how they had managed to form such an advanced society in the middle of a hostile jungle. He was fascinated by their sudden disappearance and by their religious ideas. He was intrigued by their art and by their view of the universe.

But more than anything else, Ed wanted to find places no one had seen before. So he learned to read topographical maps that show the contours of the land. This helped him pinpoint places where the ruins of cities might be located.

Ed's training paid off in 1995. He actually discovered a city when he was mapping a piece of jungle in the Central American country of Belize. He named his lost city *Ma'ax Na*, or Monkey House, because so many monkeys lived there.

In a year or two, Ed planned to head into a part of northern Guatemala called the Petén, an uninhabited, almost impenetrable region of low scrub, dense marshes, and crocodiles. Entire cities await discovery in this forbidding landscape. "I like excavating," he told me, "but I like finding cities best!"

Ed was about to get married, but he did not think marriage would change his life very much. Angela, his fiancée, understood Ed's obsession with the Maya and his love of adventure. He hoped Angela would come with him to the Petén, to help him discover another lost city.

A portion of the throne found at the Palace

A figure carved into the throne at Temple 19

30

Thrones and Tombs

The archaeologists I met at Palenque seemed to be having a great time. They worked hard all day, then met at night to share food, stories, and laughter. They were like real-life versions of the famous movie archaeologist Indiana Jones.

One day Chris Powell invited me to see the new discoveries at Temple 19. I woke early and shook out my boots before putting them on. Boots are a common hiding place for scorpions. While Ed went back into the jungle with his surveying equipment, I hiked up to Temple 19.

Chris stood under an awning of aluminum near the new discovery, the throne of Ak'al Mo' Nab. Again he got excited as he explained what he had found. Chris pointed to the artwork on the side of the beautiful throne. It was still a light reddish-brown, and I saw there the figures of Ak'al Mo' Nab and his underlords. In a few days, the throne would be dismantled and carried to an on-site museum, where it would be safe. A replica would be constructed on this spot for tourists to see.

Chris was convinced that excavations in this part of the city would also reveal the tombs of Palenque's earliest kings. Apparently there is a gap of more than two hundred years in the history of the Maya

From the throne of Ak'al Mo' Nab

city. Chris believed the last kings of Palenque may have built their temples above those of earlier kings, and that once the excavations got down far enough, crews might uncover those early kings. Chris was determined to fill the huge gaps in our knowledge. "It's all here!" he said, waving his hands around like a symphony conductor.

Chris showed me the entryway to a large, as-yet-unexplored tunnel near the site of the throne. He descended into the opening, holding a flashlight in one hand and scraping the earth with his other hand. He explained that some temples at Palenque, like King Pakal's Temple of the Inscriptions, also contain smaller tunnels, which are known as "psychoducts." These narrow shafts are about six inches wide, and they run from the king's tomb at the bottom of the temple upward a hundred feet to the open air. The Maya believed these tunnels would allow their dead kings to communicate with the living world.

Chris jumped out of the dark entryway. Soon, he and his crew would dig methodically to see where this tunnel led. He told me his goal in the next ten years was to uncover Temples 18, 18a, 19, and 20 in this part of the city, an area called the Southern Acropolis. But even after the Southern Acropolis has been completely excavated—even after another ten years of hard work—temples nearby would remain untouched. Their stories would be learned by future generations of archaeologists.

Progress is slow because the actual work of archaeology is so painstaking. The scientists don't want to miss or destroy anything. It might take one crew an entire four-month season of moving and sifting dirt to descend only a few yards. And some of the temples buried in the central part of the city are 100 feet tall!

Chris emerges from a newly excavated tunnel at Temple 19.

Snake Stories

Chris asked his crew chief, Pedro Cruz, to take me up to Temple 18, which was only a few hundred feet above Temple 19. Pedro is Manuel's older brother. He led me through the broken remnants of walls and archways up to a completely unexcavated temple.

When we arrived, I stood above future discoveries, above the tombs and altars and thrones and inscriptions of kings that lay somewhere below me, deep in the rubble.

At the top of the temple, I found a big hole amid the stones, vines, and plants. Again, looters had done their work. The blue-green feather of a parrot was lying on top of one of the stones. I picked it up, hoping it would bring me luck.

Here, only last year, Chris was bending down to observe the rocks when he noticed a fer-de-lance staring straight into his face. It was only a foot or two away. He retreated from the snake, slowly but safely. Another time, Chris looked down to see a five-foot fer-de-lance slithering over his boot. He simply waited until it passed before he moved. Chris and the other archaeologists liked to tell stories about their encounters with this deadly snake.

Like Manuel and Rogelio, Pedro spoke a language called Tzeltal, which has descended from the Maya. He also spoke Spanish. He told me that a fer-de-lance is called *nauyaca* in Tzeltal, and that if you are bitten by one you must never go to the doctor, for then you will die. Instead, a victim must immediately find a *curandero*, or local medicine man. Only curanderos, he claimed, could heal the bite of the nauyaca. This is because they are familiar with certain medicinal leaves found in the jungle.

Pedro himself knew something about the jungle vegetation. He tore a leaf from a plant that grew out of the stones. "This leaf you can chew," he said, "and you will not be thirsty."

Pedro Cruz speaks Tzeltal, a language descended from the ancient Maya.

This jungle snake looks dangerous, but its bite is not poisonous.

33

Moisés and the Mystery

Moisés' pet coatimundi

Just across a path from Ed's house, there lived an old man with white hair. His name was Moisés, which translates into English as "Moses." Moisés was the father of Alfonso Morales, the project director at Palenque. He had wandered the forest for decades, and he knew the ruins better than anyone. He knew them in his heart as well as in his mind, for he had a spiritual connection with the Maya. Moisés was a teacher, and he taught me that the spirits of the ancient Maya are alive today.

Throughout Mexico, Moisés is known as a wonderful interpreter of Palenque. Scientists from many disciplines and many countries began meeting in Moisés' house during the 1970s. Their meetings became known as the Palenque Round Table, and the knowledge gathered there enabled epigraphers to decode the Maya hieroglyphs. When the president of Mexico recently came to see the throne of Ak'al Mo' Nab, he asked Moisés to be his guide.

Bones

Moisés took Ed and me into the jungle one day. Our guide had a good sense of humor. "Ed, now that you have cut the jungle to do your mapping, I get completely lost!" he said jokingly. In reality, Moisés knew the many paths through the thick jungle as well as any town dweller knows the streets of a neighborhood. He also understood the dangers here. "The best advantage we have is to walk slowly and carefully," he said. "This is our weapon to fight the enemy."

Moisés led us to a small Maya building, out of which grew a ceiba tree. He sat down on a block of stone. He said he came here often to be alone, and to communicate with the Maya.

What happened next I cannot fully explain. Even today, when I think back on the scene, I am mystified. It started when Moisés, sitting on his stone and whittling a piece of wood with his knife, asked Ed and me to walk around the ruins of this particular house mound. He told us to stop when we felt something—anything at all. That's all he instructed us to do. He did not explain what we might be looking for.

Ed and I stepped slowly around the mound. Ed paused briefly at one corner, then continued walking. I came to the same place and noticed a disturbance in the rocks of the wall that stood before me. And I felt a little feeling. It was just a tiny something, impossible to describe. I decided to go no farther. Ed came back

to where I had stopped. He stood behind me. I was closer to the wall.

"Ready?" called Moisés.

"Yes," we said.

Moisés walked slowly up behind us, looking down at the forest floor. He came to the spot where I stood and pushed me lightly aside. Next, he surprised us by lying down on the jungle floor. On the ground, he waved his arms and felt through the leaves. Suddenly he overturned the large, flat rock I had been standing on.

Under that rock, in the half-light of the Mexican rain forest, we saw bones. Moisés picked one up and held it gingerly.

Flowers like this ginger blossom grow abundantly in the jungle.

Moisés felt through the leaves, overturning a large rock.

"Human bones," Moisés said. They apparently belonged to a man and a child. I felt a tingle run through my spine.

I do not know what it meant that I stopped on that rock, that Ed and I had somehow "found" those bones. At first I thought the ancient Maya were trying to communicate with us. Ed said that the bones should not be there. Bones disintegrate quickly in the humid, fertile climate of a jungle. If these were thousand-year-old Maya bones, it would be most mysterious indeed.

"All your life, Peter, you will wonder why it was that you came to this place," Moisés said with a wise smile. Then he put the rock back over the bones, and we left that holy shrine.

First Rain

One night I visited with Moisés across the path from the archaeologists' house. It was late, and it was about to rain for the first time in months. The jungle was dry, and the milpa fires had given off so much smoke that I had trouble photographing the ruins earlier that day. I crossed the path where Moisés' pet coatimundi, an animal that resembles a raccoon, lived in a tree. Moisés sat in a chair on his open-air patio, surrounded by six or seven dogs. The dogs were nervous, perhaps because of the coming storm. The wind grew stronger.

I sat with Moisés like a disciple while he talked about his life. He had written a book about the Maya, and he had traveled throughout the world lecturing on the subject of Palenque. He spoke many languages, and he talked to me in excellent English. In the gathering storm, Moisés said many things that seemed wise.

"I do not think that scientists are the best interpreters of Maya mysteries," he told me. "Their heads are stuffed with theory from books." Moisés' voice rose steadily against the growing storm.

"One must come fresh to the Maya, without preconceptions," he added. Then he fell silent for a moment.

"One must come fresh to the Maya, without preconceptions."

A gust of wild wind drove beetles and moths into our chests and faces. I could hardly hear Moisés' words. As the wind grew even stronger, he began to talk louder and louder, but he remained remarkably calm.

Then the thunder and lightning started. The rain came stinging across the patio, and Moisés kept talking about the Maya. The nervous dogs clustered around his feet. The biggest dog, Macho, put his muzzle on Moisés' arm and whimpered, but still Moisés talked.

I wanted to run somewhere—anywhere—to get out of the wind and the rain, but there was nowhere to go. By now the rain had plastered the thatch roof above the patio. The thunder was pounding relentlessly, and the vicious lightning exploded all around us like bombs blasting every few seconds.

I saw that Moisés was not worried, so I tried to stay calm on the outside. Inside, I was in a panic. Again, I felt that the Maya were speaking to me. They were saying something I could not understand, but it was so powerful that it connected me to the land and to the people here. It was through Moisés during that storm that I came to feel the life of the Maya. They were no longer some ancient people who had lived and died meaningless lives a thousand years ago. Instead, they were still living in the land, and in the rain and thunder. They were the very people who came down from tiny villages in the hills, like Manuel and Rogelio, to work near the ruins every day.

The rain stopped as suddenly as it had started. The wind died down, and I said good night to Moisés. I thanked the white-haired Palenque guide and crossed the path, past the sleeping coatimundi. Before I turned out the light, I recalled what Moisés had said a day earlier to a group of tourists. He told them that the archaeologists working at Palenque today—Alfonso, Chris, Ed, and others—were the heroes of our times, but added that they will not be recognized as heroes until many years in the future. "These people are preparing a magic," he said. "And someday, because of them, we will walk through the pyramids in the forest."

Before falling into a heavy sleep, I remembered something else the old guide had said. He told the tourists that Ed and his mapping crew did not realize the danger they faced every time they placed their feet among the snakes.

Carlos showed us a jungle plant that may one day be used to treat cancer.

The Village

To me, Moisés was like an elder, a wise man from a native culture. I often went to him for explanations. I told him I was having a hard time understanding the Maya. The idea of bloodletting in order to communicate with the gods, for example, seemed strange to me. I also wondered how a whole people could believe that their kings were superhuman. And most puzzling of all was the Maya view of the universe, with its many gods and spirit worlds.

When I asked Moisés about such things, he smiled like a sage. "Peter, to understand the Maya, you must listen to the people who live now in the surrounding villages. The modern Maya have a key. They speak Maya languages, and they think like the ancient Maya." His words made me eager to visit the village where Rogelio and Manuel lived.

I had only a few days left in Mexico, but I was determined to see Naranjo for myself. On the weekend, I joined Ed, Kirk, and another of Moisés' sons, Beto, for a trip to the other side of the mountain. We were led through the dense forest by a wonderful guide named Carlos, who knew all about the wildlife of the jungle and was happy to answer our questions.

A macaw, member of the parrot family

During that day trip we saw green snakes, toucans, macaws, howlers, and jungle plants used to treat cancer. We met children who were fishing with a makeshift spear gun. We came out of the thick jungle into the cut land of someone's milpa, and we saw trails of smoke in the distance above the Chiapas Mountains.

When we reached Naranjo, we found pigs wandering the streets and women and children washing their clothes in the streams. Turkeys gobbled at us from the backyards of small wooden homes. The houses were dark gray or brown, and only a few had modern metal roofs.

Every workday, from this tiny village with only a few general stores, Rogelio, Pedro, and Manuel hiked down to the ruins to make a little money. Sometimes they hiked back in pitch blackness, able to proceed only because they knew the trail so well. One dirt road ran between Naranjo and Palenque. A few trucks carried passengers back and forth, but the truck passage was too expensive for most villagers to afford, so the footpath between Naranjo and the ruins was well worn.

Moisés had said I could best learn about the Maya from the people of the villages. I asked as many questions as I could, but my visit was all too brief. I hoped someday to return and interview the old men and women of the village, who might have secrets to tell. Maybe they had as many secrets as there were stones hidden in the jungle.

Boys from the mountain village of Naranjo greeted us when we arrived.

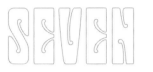

Departure

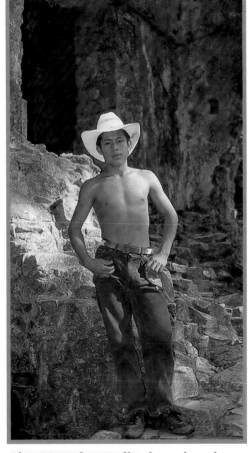

This Maya boy walks down from his home in the mountains every morning to work at Palenque.

I left Palenque early in the morning, before the tourists arrived. But first I strolled around the central plaza area, around the great palace and the Temple of the Inscriptions, and past the Southern Acropolis where so many discoveries were taking place. I reached down and grabbed a few stones. There were rocks and shards lying all around, and my son had asked me to bring him some pieces of the temple. I had told him that it was not allowed, but I thought these ordinary rocks would make good souvenirs.

While I was packing, Kirk saw the stones scattered on my bed and said, "Peter, are you sure you want to take those? A man was thrown in jail last year for buying a piece of an old pot from a tourist shop." Kirk looked concerned, but I thought nothing of it. After all, the rocks were simply discarded pieces lying in the path along with thousands or maybe millions of others.

A few minutes later, Ed barged into the room. He said, "Let me have them." For the first time since I'd arrived, he looked angry.

"Peter, you may think those are simply uninteresting rocks, but *everything* at Palenque is part of the Mexican heritage," he said. "This country takes its history very seriously."

The cool, crystal waters of L'akam Ha embody the pure mystery of the ancient Maya city.

I handed over the rocks, which I had to admit might have been shards of ancient pottery or pieces of stucco torn from city walls. As I did, I understood my error. It was not fun to be scolded, but I thanked Ed for teaching me that what I had done was wrong. At the same time, I gained new respect for the connection between ancient and modern Mexico. Palenque was indeed a living museum, and I vowed never to move another rock in such a place.

The sun came out just before I caught my plane at the Palenque airport. I remembered an experience from a few days before, when I'd gone to the waterfalls that flowed over limestone below the main part of the city. That day, I swam in the cool, clear water that bubbled out of the heart of the earth. Immersed in the crystal waters of L'akam Ha, I marveled at the dense, teeming jungle walls that surrounded me. And I felt the pure mystery that John Stephens had described long ago, when he first came upon the Maya ruins:

"All was mystery, dark, impenetrable mystery. . . ."

The Temple of the Jaguar

Today, Mexican and other North American archaeologists are working together to solve the mysteries at Palenque. Ed and his mapping crew are teaming up with excavators like Alfonso and Chris to tell the story of this lost city. Together, they are deepening our understanding of the ancient Maya, and I was most fortunate to be present in L'akam Ha at a time when great discoveries were revealed.

Yet no living human will ever know the full story of this lost civilization. It is an ongoing tale, now being told by detectives like Ed, Alfonso, and Chris, and by spiritual people like Moisés. It is also being told by the living descendants of the Maya—Rogelio, Manuel, Pedro, and others. There is much for future generations of explorers to learn.

If any reader of this book has dreamed of exploring a lost city in the jungle, or would relish the triumph of cracking a secret hieroglyphic code, or would be thrilled by excavating tombs and passageways deep within a temple, he or she should take heart. For the mystery of the Maya is unsolved, and Palenque will remain, for many centuries, a place of magic and discovery.

Glossary

Ak'al Mo' Nab (Ah-KAHL-Moh-NAHB): one of the last kings of Palenque.

aqueduct: a channel that is used to deliver drinking water, control floods, or carry away sewage.

archaeology: the scientific study of remains (such as fossil relics, artifacts, and monuments) of past human life and activities.

bloodletting: cutting oneself intentionally so that blood will flow for the purpose of inducing visions and contacting gods.

Classic period: A.D. 250–900. A time during which the Maya reached great heights in artistic, intellectual, and cultural pursuits.

coatimundi (also called coati): a tropical mammal related to the raccoon but with a longer body and tail and a long flexible snout.

curandero (koor-ahn-DAY-row): a local medicine man.

epigrapher: a scientist who studies and decodes ancient inscriptions, such as hieroglyphs.

fer-de-lance: a large and extremely venomous pit viper from Mexico, Central America and South America.

hieroglyph: a picture or symbol used to represent words or sounds.

jade: a tough, compact, typically green gemstone that takes a high polish.

machetero (mah-shay-TAY-row): a person using a machete, a long heavy knife, for cutting undergrowth.

Middleworld: In the Maya universe, the Middleworld was the Earth, a place inhabited by the living Maya. It was also considered to be a giant crocodile or turtle floating on a sea.

milpa (MIL-pah): a small farm field in Mexico or Central America that is cleared from the jungle, planted for a few seasons, and abandoned for a fresh clearing.

nauyaca (NOW-eye-YAH-kah): the Tzeltal name for the fer-de-lance, a deadly pit viper.

Pakal: (Pah-KAHL) one of Palenque's mightiest rulers, buried in the Temple of the Inscriptions.

Petén: the northernmost part of Guatemala, which was inhabited by a large population of Maya until their disappearance in the tenth century A.D.

pozol (poh-ZOHL): a mixture of white corn meal and water.

psychoduct: a narrow tunnel or stone pipe that runs from a king's tomb upward to the earth's surface. The Maya believed these tunnels allowed dead kings to communicate with the living world.

shaman: a priest who attempts to contact the spiritual world, usually during a trance.

Tzeltal (Tsel-TAHL): a group of Maya living in Chiapas who still speak their ancient dialect, also called Tzeltal.

Underworld: In Maya belief, the Underworld was the place below the Earth, where gods and the dead lived, also where the sun went at night.

Xibalbá (Shee-bahl-BAH): the Maya Underworld.

Suggested Reading

Baquedano, Elizabeth. *Aztec, Inca & Maya*. New York: Knopf, 1993.

Brown, Dale M., ed. *The Magnificent Maya*. Alexandria, Va.: Time-Life Books, 1993.

Chrisp, Peter. *The Maya*. New York: Thomsen Learning, 1994.

Coe, Michael D. *The Maya*. 5th ed., rev. New York: Thames and Hudson, 1993.

Galvin, Irene Flum. *The Ancient Maya*. Tarrytown, N.Y.: Marshall Cavendish, 1997.

Stuart, Gene S., and George E. Stuart. *Lost Kingdoms of the Maya*. Washington, D.C.: National Geographic Society, 1993.

Trout, Lawana Hooper. *The Maya*. Edited by Frank W. Porter III. New York: Chelsea House, 1991.

Author's Note

As important to me as reading books before and after making a journey are the observations I make while traipsing through jungles or following rivers. Much of the research I did for this book took place in the jungles of Chiapas. Hearing the roar of howlers and the whine of cicadas in the long, hot jungle afternoons was a big part of my exploration into the ancient culture of the Maya.

I especially enjoyed the interviews I conducted with the members of the Morales family; with Carlos the guide; with our two wonderful macheteros, Rogelio and Manuel; and with the archaeologists themselves, Ed Barnhart and Chris Powell, who told me many stories and showed me wonderful ways of looking at ruins. No feeling on earth can compare to the thrill of learning from the experts at the very location where the Maya thrived long ago. This is how the ancient mystery came alive.

A good place on the Internet for readers to learn more about Palenque and Mesoamerican cultures is *www.mesoweb.com*. To learn more about the author's explorations and books, visit *www.PeterLourie.com*.

Index